THE OUTDOORS

FLY-FISHING

by Emily Rose Oachs

FOCUS READERS

FOCUS READERS

WWW.FOCUSREADERS.COM

Focus Readers is distributed by North Star Editions:
sales@northstareditions.com | 888-417-0195

Produced for Focus Readers by Red Line Editorial.

Photographs ©: J. Michl/iStockphoto, cover, 1; Driftless Studio/iStockphoto, 4–5; duncan1890/iStockphoto, 7; skibreck/iStockphoto, 9; Fertnig/iStockphoto, 10–11, 18–19; Julieanne Birch/iStockphoto, 13; B. W. Folsom/Shutterstock Images, 15; AdShooter/iStockphoto, 16 (top left); mikedabell/iStockphoto, 16 (top right); DenBoma/iStockphoto, 16 (bottom left); Campbell Photo Studio/iStockphoto, 16 (bottom right); wwing/iStockphoto, 17 (top left); Mirek Kijewski/iStockphoto, 17 (top right); Coprid/Shutterstock Images, 17 (bottom left); abadonian/iStockphoto, 17 (bottom right); Andy Bowlin/iStockphoto, 21; J. Kendall/iStockphoto, 22–23; creighton359/iStockphoto, 25; goodluz/Shutterstock Images, 26–27; wwwarjag/Shutterstock Images, 29

ISBN
978-1-63517-229-4 (hardcover)
978-1-63517-294-2 (paperback)
978-1-63517-424-3 (ebook pdf)
978-1-63517-359-8 (hosted ebook)

Library of Congress Control Number: 2017935872

Printed in the United States of America
Mankato, MN
June, 2017

ABOUT THE AUTHOR

Emily Rose Oachs graduated as a member of Phi Beta Kappa from the University of Minnesota with a degree in communication studies. She has authored more than 50 nonfiction books for children and young adults, on topics ranging from natural disasters and biomes to geography and history. She lives and writes in Los Angeles.

TABLE OF CONTENTS

CHAPTER 1

GOING FLY-FISHING

You're standing in an icy mountain stream. You pull the tip of your fly rod over your shoulder. Then you **cast** your fly into the swift water up ahead. The stream's current drags the fly back toward you. You feel a nibble on the fly, so you pull your line to set the hook.

Fly-fishing is a great way to explore the outdoors.

As you pull, a fish leaps out of the water. It's a massive rainbow trout.

The trout tries to dart away, but you hold firm. You fight against the fish and gradually reel it in closer. Finally, the trout tires itself out. You use your net to scoop it out of the water.

People have enjoyed fly-fishing since ancient times. In 200 CE, a Roman author described people fishing with fake flies in southern Europe. Centuries later, in the early 1200s, British **anglers** fly-fished for trout and grayling along the banks of rivers and streams. During the next century, this method of fishing spread throughout the rest of Europe. By the late

An angler fishes on the Isle of Arran in Scotland in the 1800s.

1400s, fly-fishing was a popular sport among England's upper classes.

European immigrants brought the sport to North America. They fished the broad rivers of the continent's eastern coast.

By the 1950s, the rugged American West was attracting more and more fly-fishers.

For many years, people believed that fly-fishing was a sport for only the wealthy. Fly-fishing gear can be very expensive. Some high-end fly-fishing rods can cost hundreds of dollars. But there are many affordable options that work just as well. Over time, more people have learned about these other options. The sport's popularity has grown.

Fly-fishing locations have also expanded. At first, people fly-fished only in freshwater, such as rivers or streams. Later on, anglers began casting their lines in salt water, too.

An angler nets a rainbow trout.

Today anglers enjoy fly-fishing in waters around the world. Freshwater anglers often catch steelhead, trout, grayling, and salmon. Saltwater anglers often target bonefish and tarpon.

CHAPTER 2

LURES, LINES, AND LEADERS

In fly-fishing, anglers use **lures** known as flies. Flies are hooks tied with feathers, hair, yarn, and other materials. They are made to attract and catch fish. Flies look like the insects or small animals that fish eat. Each fly is designed for a different situation. Some flies float on the water's surface. Other flies sink into the water.

Anglers often carry their flies in a tackle box.

Anglers usually carry a variety of flies with them.

An angler's long fly rod launches the fly out onto the water. Fly rods also help anglers set the hook in a fish's mouth and **land** the fish. A fly rod must be both strong and flexible. This allows the rod

TYING FLIES

Thousands of different fly patterns exist. Anglers can purchase flies from fly shops or online. Yet for many anglers, the process of tying flies can be as relaxing and enjoyable as fishing. Catching fish on flies they have tied themselves can be one of the sport's greatest rewards.

Most fly-fishing rods are between 7 feet (2.1 m) and 11 feet (3.4 m) long.

to bend under the weight of a large fish without breaking.

A reel at the base of the rod stores the line. Reels can hold as much as 100 feet (30 m) of line.

Fly-fishing line is relatively heavy. Its weight helps push the fly forward when an angler is casting. This allows the angler to send the fly farther out onto the water.

A leader connects the fly to the line. The leader gently drops the fly onto the water's surface. It also helps the fly move in the water. The leader is lightweight and difficult to see. Anglers use the leader to copy the natural movements of a fish's prey. They try to trick fish into thinking that the flies are food.

Anglers use other helpful gear, too. Sometimes anglers must wade into the water to cast to a certain area. Tall,

This fishing vest has a patch of fleece where anglers can store flies.

waterproof pants called waders help them stay dry. Other anglers wear vests with many pockets. The pockets provide space for anglers to keep tackle close at hand. Some anglers also carry **creels** for storing the fish they catch.

FLY-FISHING SUPPLIES

☐ 1. Creel

☐ 2. Flies

☐ 3. Fly line

☐ 4. Fly rod and reel

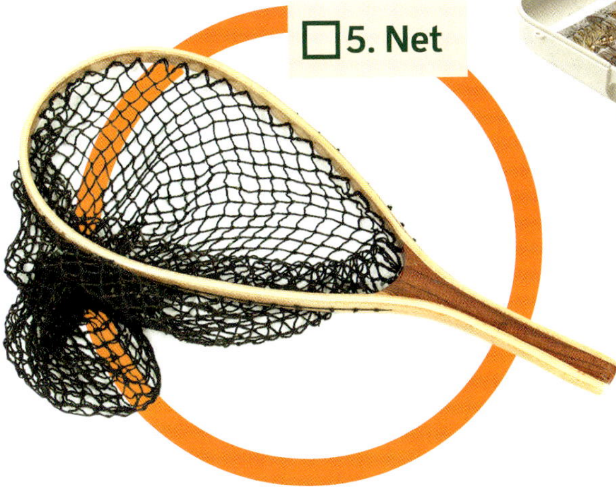

☐ 5. Net

☐ 6. Tackle box

☐ 7. Vest

☐ 8. Waders

CHAPTER 3

LANDING A FISH

Choosing a good location is a key part of fly-fishing. Anglers look for places where fish are likely to feed. Weedy areas and water near overhanging plants and trees are good places to find fish. So are areas behind boulders or near fallen logs. Fish also tend to swim near **eddies** and other areas with slower currents.

Wearing camouflage clothing helps anglers blend in with the fish's habitat.

These calmer waters help keep fish from wasting energy.

Anglers must approach their fishing spots carefully. Bright clothing or loud noises can frighten fish. Anglers often wear clothes that blend in with the fish's **habitat**. They may even crouch or crawl to the water's edge.

PLAYING A FISH

Fish often try to free themselves from the hook. Anglers must fight against a fish until it tires itself out. This is called playing a fish. When playing a fish, anglers keep their lines tight. They keep the tips of their rods up. Once the fish is exhausted, the angler can land it.

Many anglers fish for trout.

When a fish bites, the angler quickly pulls the line tight. This sets the hook in the fish's mouth. Then the angler begins reeling the fish in closer. A net can help the angler scoop up and land the fish.

CHAPTER 4

STAYING SAFE

Fly-fishing is a great way to enjoy the outdoors. But it also brings some risks. A fly's hook is sharp enough to pierce a person's skin. Before casting, anglers should look for people nearby. This helps them avoid hooking others or getting hooked themselves.

It is important to be careful when wading.

Fast-flowing water can knock over an angler. Underwater rocks may be slippery. If people stumble and fall into the water, a strong current could sweep them away. The cold water could also cause them to get **hypothermia**. To prevent this, anglers should wade slowly and cautiously.

WEATHER SAFETY

Anglers must keep an eye on the weather, too. On clear days, anglers should wear sunscreen, hats, and sunglasses. Rain jackets and other waterproof clothing will keep them warm and dry in the rain. If a thunderstorm looms, anglers should stop fishing and seek shelter immediately. Their fly rods can conduct electricity if struck by lightning.

Wading boots help anglers keep their footing on rocky bottoms.

Walking sticks help anglers maintain their balance in the water. Secure wading belts keep water out of waders if anglers fall.

A first aid kit helps anglers care for minor injuries. People fishing in remote areas should also pack a blanket, a compass, and extra food. This helps them be prepared in case of an emergency.

CHAPTER 5

PROTECTING HABITATS

Governments create fly-fishing laws to help with **conservation**. By following these laws, anglers can help protect the health of fish and their habitats. Some laws allow people to fly-fish only at certain times. Some limit how many fish anglers can keep. Others require anglers to only keep fish above a certain size.

It is important to handle fish gently.

Anglers must release any fish that are smaller than this size. This helps make sure young fish can grow into adults and reproduce.

Fly-fishing laws also require most anglers to purchase a fishing license. Part of the money from license sales is used to help with conservation. The government uses this money to care for the environment. The money may go toward cleaning rivers and lakes.

While fishing, anglers should be careful not to disturb the habitats of fish and other animals. They should clean up their own litter and any litter left by others.

Anglers make sure a fish has fully recovered before letting it go back into the water.

Many anglers also choose to practice catch-and-release fishing. These anglers do not keep the fish they catch. Instead, they carefully unhook the fish. Then they gently return the fish to the water. Catch-and-release fishing helps ensure that there will be enough fish for other anglers to catch in the future.

FOCUS ON

FLY-FISHING

Write your answers on a separate piece of paper.

1. Write a sentence that describes the key ideas from Chapter 5.
2. What do you think would be the most difficult part of fly-fishing? Why?
3. What piece of equipment stores the fly line?

    A. the reel
    B. the creel
    C. the leader

4. What might happen if anglers kept fish that were below the size limit?

    A. The fish population would increase because the fish would not have to compete for food.
    B. The fish population would decrease because fewer fish would survive to become adults.
    C. The fish population would stay the same because fish size and numbers are not related.

Answer key on page 32.

GLOSSARY

anglers
People who fish with a rod, reel, and line.

cast
To use a fishing rod to throw a line with bait or a lure out over the water.

conservation
The careful protection of plants, animals, and natural resources so they are not lost or wasted.

creels
Baskets that anglers use to hold their fish.

eddies
Currents of water that move in a circle or flow the opposite way from the main current.

habitat
The type of place where plants or animals normally grow or live.

hypothermia
The loss of body heat to a level much lower than normal.

land
To bring in a hooked fish from the water.

lures
Types of artificial bait used to attract and catch fish.

TO LEARN MORE

BOOKS

Hamilton, S. L. *Fly Fishing*. Minneapolis: Abdo Publishing, 2015.

Omoth, Tyler. *Fly Fishing for Kids*. North Mankato, MN: Capstone Press, 2013.

Pendergast, George. *Fly Fishing*. New York: Gareth Stevens Publishing, 2015.

NOTE TO EDUCATORS

Visit **www.focusreaders.com** to find lesson plans, activities, links, and other resources related to this title.

INDEX

Answer Key: 1. Answers will vary; **2.** Answers will vary; **3.** A; **4.** B